NO - - ᴎ

CALICO ILLUSTRATED CLASSICS

Charlotte Brontë's

Jane Eyre

ADAPTED BY: Jan Fields
ILLUSTRATED BY: Eric Scott Fisher

magic
Wagon

visit us at www.abdopublishing.com

Published by Magic Wagon, a division of the ABDO Group,
8000 West 78th Street, Edina, Minnesota 55439. Copyright
© 2012 by Abdo Consulting Group, Inc. International copyrights
reserved in all countries. All rights reserved. No part of this
book may be reproduced in any form without written permission
from the publisher.

Calico Chapter Books™ is a trademark and logo of Magic Wagon.

Printed in the United States of America, Melrose Park, Illinois.
052011
092011

 This book contains at least 10% recycled materials.

Original text by Charlotte Brontë
Adapted by Jan Fields
Illustrated by Eric Scott Fisher
Edited by Stephanie Hedlund and Rochelle Baltzer
Cover and interior design by Abbey Fitzgerald

Library of Congress Cataloging-in-Publication Data

Fields, Jan.
  Charlotte Bronte's Jane Eyre / adapted by Jan Fields ; illustrated by
Eric Scott Fisher.
     p. cm. -- (Calico illustrated classics)
  ISBN 978-1-61641-615-7
  [1. Orphans--Fiction. 2. Governesses--Fiction. 3. Great Britain--
History--19th century--Fiction.] I. Fisher, Eric Scott, ill. II. Bronte,
Charlotte, 1816-1855. Jane Eyre. III. Title.
  PZ7.F479177Ck 2011
  [Fic]--dc22
                                        2011002733

Table of Contents

CHAPTER 1

The Ghost

The cold winter wind had brought gloom and rain. I was glad of it. I never liked long walks on chilly afternoons and the bad weather saved me from one.

Eliza, John, and Georgiana played around their mama in the drawing room. I was not invited. Mrs. Reed insisted I keep my distance from her and her darlings.

I preferred my own company anyway. I slipped into the breakfast room and sat cross-legged in the window seat with a book in my lap.

Then the door flew open. "Madam Mope!" cried John Reed. "Where is she?"

I had drawn the curtain when I slipped into the window seat. It was unlikely John would have found me, but Eliza put her head in at the door and said, "She is in the window seat."

I came out immediately, as I had no wish to be dragged out. John snatched away my book.

"You have no money and you ought to beg and not live here with gentlemen's children like us. I'll teach you not to touch my things. Everything in this house is mine!"

He insisted I go and stand by the door. I went. He flung the heavy book at me and it knocked me down. I struck my head on the door and it began to bleed. The blood and the pain opened the door to the anger in me. The hot anger that had longed to come out for all the years I had been trapped in that cold house.

"Wicked boy!" I said. "You are an evil bully."

He ran at me then and grabbed my hair. I felt a drop or two of blood trickle down my neck and I fought back wildly. John screamed and Mrs. Reed rushed into the room with our nursemaid Bessie and another maid, Abbot.

"Take her away to the red room," Mrs. Reed said. "Lock her in there."

I was dragged upstairs and locked in. The red room was kept clean but never used anymore. The servants were a bit afraid of it, and I was terrified. This was the very room where Mr. Reed had died many years before.

Mr. Reed was my uncle. He was the one who insisted I be brought to live with them when my parents died of typhus fever. On his deathbed, he had made Mrs. Reed swear to raise me as her own.

It was that promise that froze my blood now. Mrs. Reed had surely broken it. I lived there, but she hated me and her children tormented me. Would Mr. Reed now see their treatment and come back from the grave? The very thought of the cold hand of comfort from a ghost made my heart race in my chest.

The room was dark from the cloudy day. Bessie had left me a lantern and the flickering glow cast shadows that danced on the walls like a vision from another world. I heard rushing in my head and knew it to be wings. I felt something near me.

I ran to the door and flung myself against it kicking and pounding and screaming.

"Miss Eyre, are you ill?" Bessie asked when she opened the door.

"Let me out," I begged. "I saw a light. A ghost."

"What is this?" Mrs. Reed stormed along the corridor. "I gave orders that Jane Eyre should be left in the red room until I came to her myself."

"She screamed so loud, ma'am," Bessie pleaded.

"Oh Aunt, have pity! Forgive me!" I begged. "I cannot endure it!"

"Silence," she snapped. "You will stay here an hour longer until you can be perfectly still." She thrust me back into the room and locked me in.

Then with my back against the door and the darkness of the room closing in around me, I passed out.

I awoke in my own bed. Bessie stood nearby with the man who was sometimes called when the servants were sick.

"Do you know who I am?" he asked.

I nodded and said, "Mr. Lloyd."

"Do you have any pain? Can you tell me what happened to make you ill?"

"She had a fall," Bessie said.

"I was knocked down," I told him, insulted by the suggestion that I was a clumsy child who fell down. "But that didn't make me ill. I was shut up in a dark room where there is a ghost."

"A ghost!" Mr. Lloyd said with a smile. "You are afraid of ghosts?"

"Of Mr. Reed's ghost I am. None of the servants will go into that room in the dark, but they shut me up in there. It was cruel."

Mr. Lloyd continued to ask questions. I told him that I was an orphan with cousins who abused me and an aunt who punished me for the bad behavior of her own children.

"Have you any relatives besides Mrs. Reed?" he asked.

"I don't know. Aunt Reed said I might have some poor relations called *Eyre*. But she knew nothing about them."

"If you had such relatives, would you like to go live with them?"

I thought about that. I knew little of being poor, only what my cousins said. I believed all the poor to be ragged, dirty, hungry, cold, and given to terrible acts. I was not brave enough to escape the Reeds that way, so I shook my head.

"Aunt Reed said they are all beggars. I wouldn't like to beg," I said.

"Would you like to go to school?" Mr. Lloyd asked.

I thought about that. John went to school and hated it, but I did not let that trouble me.

John liked very few things. I knew you learned things at school and I liked that idea.

"Yes," I finally replied.

"Well, let us see what happens," he said. "The child could use a change of air and scene." Then he left to speak to Mrs. Reed. Afterward, I learned that I would be sent to school as soon as possible.

CHAPTER 2

Lowood Institute

Weeks passed. Mrs. Reed insisted her darlings stay far away from me, so my life improved. At one point John tried to bully me, but I would not accept such treatment and fought back.

When John ran howling to his mother, she only scolded him, "I told you not to go near her. She is not worthy of notice."

At that, I cried out, "They are not fit to associate with me!"

Mrs. Reed fairly flew up the stairs at me and nearly hurled me into the nursery. Again, my tongue would not be silent.

"What would Uncle Reed say to you, if he were alive?" I demanded.

"What?" she whispered, her face fearful.

"Uncle Reed is in heaven. He can see what you do. So can my papa and mama. They know how you lock me up. They know you wish me dead!"

Mrs. Reed shook me roughly and stormed out of the nursery. After that I was kept even farther from her and my cousins. I was rarely noticed and that alone made my life better.

Then, in January, a visitor came and I was called downstairs. Mrs. Reed was in the breakfast room with a tall, grim man named Mr. Brocklehurst.

"Her size is small," he said.

"She is ten years old," Mrs. Reed said. "Old enough for your school, I believe."

"Jane Eyre, are you a good child?"

Mrs. Reed said that I was not. She told him I was prone to lying.

The tall man frowned at me. "Do you know where the wicked go after death?"

"To hell," I said.

"What must you do to avoid it?" he asked.

"I must keep in good health and not die."

Clearly he did not like that answer. "You have a wicked heart," Mr. Brocklehurst said. Then he gave me a little book about a child who lies and suffers for it. He turned to Mrs. Reed and said, "Deceit is a sad fault in a child. I will speak to the teachers so that she may be watched."

Soon after this, Mr. Brocklehurst left. I was furious that Mrs. Reed had ruined my chance to make a fresh start at school.

"I am not deceitful," I said to her, my voice low and fierce. "This book is about what happens to liars. You may give it to your children and read it yourself."

"Is that all?" she asked coldly.

"If anyone asks how I liked you and how you treated me, I will tell them the truth," I said. "You think I have no feelings, but it is you who are without feelings. When I begged for mercy you thrust me back into that terrible room. People think you are a good woman, but you are bad and hardhearted."

As I finished that speech, I felt free. I was free of pretending and trying to get along in that horrible house. I saw nothing else of the family before I was sent on my way to school. The journey lasted a full day, and I was exhausted when we finally arrived.

I was met by a teacher's helper named Mrs. Miller. She bundled me along through dark corridors and into a wide, long room filled with tables. Girls of all ages sat at the tables, studying by candlelight.

"Monitors, collect the lesson books and put them away," Mrs. Miller called as she seated me at a table near the door. "Fetch the supper trays."

I was given water and a thin oaten cake. I was too tired to eat, but I drank the water. After that, we were soon off to bed. A bitterly cold morning came early. We washed and dressed, shivering all the while.

When time came for breakfast, I was very hungry from not eating the day before. We were each given a bowl of burned porridge. In my hunger, I was able to eat several spoons before the horrible taste made me gag. Most of the girls couldn't manage even a single spoonful.

Then lessons began. I was sent to sit with the youngest class. After we had been at lessons a while, the superintendent of Lowood entered the room. I thought her very beautiful with kind eyes.

"I heard you had a poor breakfast," Miss Temple said. "I have ordered that a lunch of bread and cheese be served to all."

The teachers looked surprised and concerned.

"It is done on my responsibility," she assured them.

After we enjoyed our lunch, we were ordered into our cloaks and sent into the garden. The weather was cold and wet, but the stronger of the girls ran around playing games. Others huddled together for warmth.

No one had spoken to me or even seemed to notice me. I was lonely but not unhappy. I spotted a girl reading on a stone bench. As I loved to read, I walked closer.

"Is your book interesting?" I asked.

"I like it," she said, looking up at me in a quiet, friendly way.

I looked down at the book. It seemed to have a great many words and did not look so interesting to me. She was about to turn back to her book when I asked, "Can you tell me about that writing?" I pointed at the words carved into the side of the building.

"Lowood Institute is this school," she said. "It's a charity school for educating orphans. It was begun by Naomi Brocklehurst and is now run by her son. He is a clergyman."

She answered all my questions patiently, telling me the names of the teachers and their subjects. She agreed that Miss Temple was the kindest person she knew. Then she sent me on my way so she could return to her book.

The rest of the day passed in lessons, studying, and poor food. The only thing that stood out to me was when the history teacher punished the kind girl from the garden.

"Helen Burns, where is your mind?" the angry teacher asked.

The girl was forced to stand in disgrace in the middle of the classroom. I didn't know how she could stand it, but she seemed very brave.

Finally my first day at Lowood was over. And though I could have wished for better food, I found the day decidedly more pleasant than any I had spent with the Reeds.

CHAPTER 3

Miss Temple's Kindness

My second day began as the first, except the cold had frozen the water in our washbasin. Our morning porridge wasn't burned, though I wished I had more of it.

We all took lessons in the same room. So, I often noticed that the reading girl was a special object of one teacher's bad temper.

"Helen Burns, turn your toes out," Miss Scatcherd cried. "Stand up straight and draw in your chin."

The worst scolding fell when the teacher caught sight of Helen's hands. "You dirty girl," she shrieked. "You didn't clean your nails this morning!"

How unfair, I thought. *No one would wash in water frozen to ice.* But Helen never looked cross. She never cried. She answered the teacher politely no matter what was said.

At play hour, I found Helen reading. "Do you ever wish you could leave Lowood?" I asked her. "Miss Scatcherd is so cruel to you."

"No, of course not," she said. "I am here to learn. Miss Scatcherd is here to correct my faults."

"I wouldn't allow it," I said hotly.

"It is your duty," Helen said. "It's silly to refuse to correct your faults."

"But what faults could you have?" I asked. She seemed very good to me.

"I am careless and my mind wanders so easily," she said.

I could not imagine how Helen could stand the cruel teacher. I hated Mrs. Reed and my cousins for their cruelty. And I would hate Miss Scatcherd if she treated me as she did Helen. I told Helen about all the cruel things I had suffered from the Reeds.

"You hold so tightly to your list of wrongs," she said. "This world is only a passing thing. Look ahead, Jane."

I thought often of what Helen said as the winter passed slowly into spring. I wasn't certain I wished to embrace her view of life, but I admired her for it. The warmer weather brought joy to us all. The days blended together. Only one really stood out.

About three weeks after my arrival, Mr. Brocklehurst had come to visit the school. He wanted to be certain we were all properly miserable. He scolded Miss Temple for giving us an extra lunch when our breakfast was spoiled. He insisted several of the girls have their hair cut short. He was especially horrified at the sight of one girl with a head of natural curls.

"We are not to conform to nature," he snapped. "I will have no curls, no braids, no fancy hair on these girls." His scolding was interrupted by the arrival of his wife and daughters. They wore velvet, silk, and fur and their hair was done up in curls. Clearly Mr. Brocklehurst's view of girls did not include his own family.

Throughout this visit, I had sat well back among my class and held my slate in front of my face. Somehow I managed to snap my slate right out of my hands. It crashed to the floor and broke. Every eye turned to me then.

Mr. Brocklehurst recognized me at once. He insisted I be set upon a high stool. "Do you see this girl?" he asked everyone in the room. "It is my duty to warn you that you must shun this girl. Be on your guard against her. This girl is a liar!"

I heard gasps in response to his words. He then ordered that I was to remain on the stool for a half hour and that no one was to speak to me for the rest of that day. Then, he left with his family. I could hardly bear the shame.

Finally, Helen Burns came to me, carrying coffee and bread. "Come and eat," she said.

I could not. I was choked with my sorrow.

"Why do you talk to me? Everybody hates me for being a liar," I said.

"No, Jane," she said gently. "No one here likes Mr. Brocklehurst. I am certain most of the girls feel sorry for you."

Just as she said this, Miss Temple entered the room to collect me. She brought Helen along as well. We went to Miss Temple's own room and she offered me something to eat. I could barely look at her in my sorrow. She asked me why.

"Because I have been wrongly accused," I said. "And everybody will think me wicked."

"We shall think only what you prove to be," Miss Temple said. "Continue to act as a good girl and we will think well of you."

Then Miss Temple asked where Mr. Brocklehurst had heard that I was a liar. I told her about Mrs. Reed. I was careful to tell my experience as calmly as I could. I finished by telling the part Mr. Lloyd had played in getting me to school.

"I will write to Mr. Lloyd," Miss Temple said. "If he agrees with what you just told me, I will be certain you are publicly cleared. To me, you are already clear. I do not think you a liar."

In that moment, her kindness was the most wonderful thing I had ever known. I would have stayed there with her and Helen forever.

I even managed to eat a bit of the cakes and tea that Miss Temple offered.

Miss Temple was as good as her word. A week later she assembled the whole school and announced that she had investigated and found me clear of the charge of lying. The teachers all shook hands with me and several kissed my cheek. After Miss Temple's kindness I set to work at the school with fresh energy.

I progressed so quickly that I was able to take classes for older students in French and drawing. I came to feel at home at my new school. And I learned that even poor food and bitter weather could not make me miss life with my aunt, no matter what luxuries they had.

CHAPTER
4
A New Position

Spring settled in and Lowood bloomed. I often took walks and enjoyed the hills and trails around the school. But the spring rain brought dampness as well as disease.

Scant food and a harsh winter had left many of the girls thin and frail. When the typhus fever struck, they were the first to fall ill. Eventually, forty-five of the eighty students were too sick to rise from their beds. The teachers were so busy tending the sick and dying that classes stopped. The healthier girls with some family or friends packed up and left.

So while the land around Lowood grew more alive and beautiful each day, the gloom inside the school grew darker. The weakest girls died from the fever. Helen Burns was ill as well, though not with typhus. Instead, Helen had tuberculosis.

I thought Helen merely had a cough and would soon recover. Then one day, Miss Temple carried her out to the garden. Helen was wrapped in blankets and I was not allowed to go near her. I knew then that she was very ill.

In June, I saw the doctor leaving and the nurse looking sad and tired. I ran up to her and asked, "How is Helen Burns?"

"Very poorly," she said.

"Did the doctor see her?" I asked. "What did he say?"

"He says she'll not be here long," the nurse said. "She's in Miss Temple's room, but you must stay away and be well."

After we were sent to bed that night, I crept down to Miss Temple's room. I found a small bed where Helen slept. She was very pale and thin, but smiled when she saw me.

"Can it be you, Jane?" Helen whispered.

I thought then, *she can't be going to die. How could she speak so sweetly and calmly if she were dying?* I kissed her on the forehead and her skin was cold. "I came to see you. I heard you were very ill."

"You came to bid me good-bye," Helen said. "I think you are just in time."

"Are you going somewhere?"

"Yes, I am going home, to the best home of all," she said.

I cried out that she must not, but she only told me to climb under the quilt. "Your feet will be cold," she said. So I did and we nestled close.

"I am very happy," she said. "My mind is at rest. Sleep now and don't worry. Are you warm enough?"

I said I was and we both fell asleep. I awoke to discover someone was carrying me. It was the nurse. Helen Burns had died in the night.

She was buried in a nearby churchyard. So many students died at Lowood that year that

public attention turned to the school. The school's faults could not be hidden. Poor food, bad water, and inadequate heat and clothing had all played their part in the deaths.

The uproar led to changes. Mr. Brocklehurst still tended the school's funds, but he was strictly watched. The school improved. I remained there for eight more years. My life was uniform but not unhappy. I excelled in my studies and enjoyed them. Eventually I became a teacher there for two years.

Miss Temple stayed at the school those eight years and I valued her friendship. Then she married a clergyman and moved to a distant country. From the day she left, the school was not the same for me. I no longer wanted to remain, and I decided I wanted to find service elsewhere.

I decided to use the newspaper to advertise for a position. My advertisement was simple. I stated that I was seeking a private family position to teach children under fourteen. As

I was barely eighteen, I thought it wise to put in an age limit. I mentioned that I had taught basic lessons for the last two years and was qualified to teach French, drawing, and music.

From this ad, I received one reply from a Mrs. Fairfax of Thornfield. In it, she asked for references. The position would involve teaching a little girl under ten and would pay thirty pounds a year.

As Mrs. Reed was noted as my only family, a notice was sent to her of my desire to leave Lowood. She replied that she had no interest in whatever I did. I was given formal leave and references from the school. Thus, I was soon able to pack my trunk and prepare for my new adventure.

Before I could leave, I received the most amazing guest. I was called downstairs, where I saw an older woman dressed as a servant from a well-to-do home. The woman smiled at the sight of me and I knew her then.

"Bessie!" I called. I hugged her in delight.

Then I saw a small boy standing near the fire. "That is my little boy," Bessie said.

"Then you are married?" I said, smiling.

"Yea, nearly five years. I married Robert Leaven, the coachman. I have a little girl, too. I named her Jane."

I asked about my aunt's family and learned Miss Georgiana and her sister fought constantly. John had not come out quite as his mother hoped, and he spent a great deal of his mother's money.

"And what brings you here?" I asked. "Surely not Mrs. Reed."

"Oh no," Bessie said. "I had heard there was a letter from the school here about you taking a position. I thought I would just hurry over and visit before you were sent so far away."

She clapped with delight when I played the piano for her. "I always said you could surpass them all in learning," Bessie said. "You are quite a lady, Miss Jane!"

Then Bessie told me the most surprising thing of all. Four years before, a Mr. Eyre had come to see my aunt to ask about me.

"Mrs. Reed called him a sneaking tradesman," Bessie said. "But he looked quite a gentleman. I believe he was your father's brother. He was going to Madeira."

Bessie left soon after and a few days later, I left as well to start a new life.

Thornfield Hall

The trip to Thornfield was long and exhausting. I passed much of the time trying to imagine Mrs. Fairfax in my mind. I pictured a very wealthy elderly woman, but revised my thoughts slightly when the servant and carriage that picked me up in Millcote were very plain. I liked the new idea better, as my experience with fine people had been so unpleasant.

We passed a church just before we passed through a pair of gates and finally reached Thornfield Hall.

A maidservant led me into a small, snug room. An elderly lady in a black silk gown sat knitting by a cheerful fire. A large cat sat at her feet. In all, it was the perfect picture of home. The old lady got up and promptly came forward to meet me.

"How do you do, my dear? Oh, your hands are cold. Come and sit by the fire." She called the maid to bring me tea. Then she called for my luggage to be carried to my room. In all, everything in her manner was warmer and kinder than I had expected.

She told me she was so happy that I had come, as she often felt lonely in the great house.

"Little Adèle makes the house alive, of course," Mrs. Fairfax said. "And now that you are here, I shall be quite happy."

After my brief meal, the kind lady sent me right off to bed. My room was lovely and I felt certain I would be happy in my new position. I slept well and arose early. As I walked down the stairs, I met Mrs. Fairfax.

"I see you are an early riser," she said. "How do you like Thornfield?"

"It's beautiful."

"It is a pretty place, though I wish Mr. Rochester would come more often," she said. "A fine home needs its master."

"Mr. Rochester?" I asked. "Who is he?"

"The owner of Thornfield," she said. "You did not know?"

I did not, but I soon learned. Mrs. Fairfax was not my employer. She was Mr. Rochester's housekeeper and a distant relative of the family. And the child I would be teaching was Mr. Rochester's ward. And at that, the child appeared, followed by her nurse.

"Good morning, Miss Adèle," said Mrs. Fairfax. "Come and speak to the woman who is to teach you."

"*C'est la gouvernante?*" she asked, turning to her nurse.

"*Mais oui,*" the nurse confirmed.

I quickly learned that neither Adèle nor her nurse spoke a great deal of English. That was not a problem for me as I spoke French well. I introduced myself to the child in French and she smiled in delight. Then she launched into a long tale of her trip to England with her nurse Sophie.

I soon learned that young Adèle loved to talk. She was far more inclined to chatter than most English children, and she often let her imagination run away with her. She was sweet and affectionate, though a bit spoiled. I learned her mother was a French singer.

We began her instruction right away. I found Adèle eager to please but not fond of sitting still. I decided to keep lessons confined to the short morning hours to best suit her ability and temperament.

During my free time, I helped out around the house when asked. Even that left me with restless time on my hands. Mrs. Fairfax took me on a tour of the house, which I enjoyed. Though they kept only a small staff, the house was beautifully maintained and neat.

Then on the third floor, I heard a cold, hollow laugh. It was low but distinct. When

I asked Mrs. Fairfax what made the sound, she told me that another servant had her rooms on that floor.

"Grace Poole often sews in one of these rooms. Sometimes Leah is with her. They can be noisy together," Mrs. Fairfax said.

The laugh sounded again and I wondered what kind of conversation could lead to such an odd, unhealthy laugh. I heard the laugh many times in the coming days and I often wondered what sort of person this Grace Poole must be.

Though I found my position enjoyable, I continued to grow restless in my quiet hours. One day, I offered to carry some letters to the small village of Hay that lay just two miles from Thornfield.

Winter lay cold and hard on the land around me. The road from Thornfield Hall to Hay was all uphill. When I had climbed halfway up, I stopped to rest on a low wall. I was startled out of my thoughts by the sound of hooves.

First, a large black-and-white dog raced by me without a glance in my direction. Then a tall horse passed. Suddenly, the horse slipped on the icy road. Man and horse went down. The dog rushed to the man's side, barking wildly.

I stood and ran to the man's side as the horse climbed back to its feet. "Are you injured, sir? Can I do anything?" I asked.

"Just stand out of my way," he demanded. Then he snapped at the barking dog, "Quiet, Pilot."

I stepped away. The man stood and limped to the rock wall. He was a strong-looking man of about thirty-five. He had a dark face with stern features that no one would call handsome.

"If you are hurt and want help, sir, I can fetch someone from either Thornfield Hall or from Hay," I said.

"It is only a sprain," he said, his voice rough. "You may go."

"I cannot think of leaving you, sir, unless I am sure you are fit to mount your horse," I replied.

He frowned and asked me where I was from. I told him that I had come from Thornfield Hall and was going to Hay to post letters. He then asked me what I was doing at Thornfield.

"I am the governess," I replied.

"Ah, right, I had forgotten." He looked me over closely, then he finally allowed me to help him to his horse. He mounted with a clear show of pain. "Thank you. Now make haste with the letter to Hay and return as fast as you can."

He rode away and I completed my errand with the comfortable feeling of something interesting having happened. When I returned to Thornfield, I found the large black-and-white dog lying on the rug in Mrs. Fairfax's sitting room.

"Pilot?" I said.

The dog stood, his tail wagging. Mrs. Fairfax came in behind me.

"Whose dog is this?" I asked.

"He belongs to the master," she said. "He just arrived, but he had a fall in the lane. I am certain it is only a sprain, but we have sent for the doctor." Then she hurried off to collect tea for Mr. Rochester. I drifted upstairs to my room with more interesting new things to think about.

CHAPTER 6

Fire!

The next day, I woke to a Thornfield Hall that was much changed. Everyone buzzed with excitement over the master's visit, and I could not get Adèle to concentrate on her studies. In the afternoon, Adèle and I were called to join Mr. Rochester for tea.

When I entered the fine drawing room, I saw that Mr. Rochester did not look any more cheerful when reclining on a couch with his foot on a cushion than he had when sprawled on the road. As he sat in silence, Mrs. Fairfax served tea.

Adèle stood quietly for a few moments before speaking to Mr. Rochester in rapid French. "Do you have a small gift for Miss Eyre in the package that is coming?" she asked.

He frowned at me. "Do you expect a present, Miss Eyre? Are you fond of presents?"

"I have little experience with them," I said. "They are generally thought pleasant things. But as a stranger, I would hardly expect to receive one."

Then he quizzed me on my qualifications as governess and on my family. I named my skills calmly and told him I had no family. He asked to see my drawings and I brought them.

I often painted from my own imagination, and I suppose my choices were odd. I had painted the night sky like a woman looking out on the world. And I had painted a snow-white arm cast up on a beach from a shipwreck. Nearby a seagull held a jewel stolen from the drowned seafarer. Looking back, I know my drawings were hardly girlish.

After looking over my work, Mr. Rochester bid us an abrupt good night. For several days after that, I saw little of him. Gentlemen called on business most days. We were not invited to another tea time until Adèle's gifts finally arrived. Her box contained small dolls and a lovely new dress. She was delighted.

Mr. Rochester treated the child gruffly but not unkindly. He insisted I sit close by him.

"Do you think me handsome, Miss Eyre?" he asked.

"No, sir."

"You are interesting," he said with a laugh. "You spend so much time looking at the carpet, but you observe everything around you like a bird. Then when you open your mouth, the most amazing things come out."

"I beg your pardon, sir," I said.

He waved away the apology. "Your view of my appearance was no mistake. I am content with it. I do believe you will do me good, Miss Eyre." We chatted on the oddest subjects before he was willing to let us retire for the night.

We met again several days later when I had taken Adèle on a walk. My young student immediately ran to play with Pilot. Mr. Rochester watched her.

"Her mother was very beautiful and I thought I loved her," he said quietly. "I gave her many things and she gave me this child."

"Adèle is your daughter?" I asked.

"I thought so once," he said. "But then I learned she had many who loved her. I discovered her with a young French aristocrat. They were laughing together about me and about my foolishness. That ended my feelings for Adèle's mother."

"Then why is the child with you?" I asked.

He shrugged. "Perhaps to remind me not to be foolish. I have watched her closely. I see nothing that hints that she could be my daughter. I think she is not. But her mother is gone and she needs a home. Perhaps you will help her grow into a woman who is not like her mother? Or does my story offend you and make you want to leave Thornfield?"

"I shall care even more for Adèle, knowing she needs my love," I said.

Mr. Rochester nodded and soon left. When the day was over and I went to bed, I found thoughts of Mr. Rochester's story kept me awake. Suddenly, I heard an odd sound in the hall. I wondered if it might be Pilot, pacing the halls as he sometimes did.

Then I heard a sound against my door, like clawed fingers drawn across the wood. This sound was followed by a laugh, deep and low, right at my keyhole. Something gurgled and moaned. Then steps ran away down the hall.

I quickly dressed and crept out into the hall. The air was hazy and smelled of smoke. I rushed down the hall to seek the source and found Mr. Rochester's door open a crack. Smoke drifted out.

I rushed into the room and found Mr. Rochester's bed curtains were on fire. "Wake! Wake!" I cried, shaking him. I could not wake

him and wondered if the smoke had already begun its work on him.

I grabbed the water jug and threw it on the flames. Then I emptied the washbasin of water on them as well. Finally, I ran to my room and fetched my full pitcher and added that to totally quench the flames.

Much of the water splashed over onto Mr. Rochester. He finally woke, demanding to know why I was trying to drown him. I explained what I had done and he insisted I not call anyone to the room.

"Sit down here," he said, leading me to a chair. "Remain here as still as a mouse. I must check something on the third floor. Don't move or call anyone."

I waited as he asked and finally he returned, looking pale and gloomy. "Was it Grace Poole, sir?" I asked.

He looked at me in surprise. I explained that I had heard the servant laughing many times.

"Just so," he said. "Grace Poole. I shall think about what to do with her. Meanwhile, say nothing of this. Return to your room and I will sleep the rest of the night in the library."

"Good night," I said, turning to go.

"What?" he exclaimed. "Are you leaving?"

"You told me to go, sir," I said.

"But not without a word. You have saved my life. At least shake hands." He held out his hand and I gave him mine. He held my hand for a time in both of his.

"I owe you a great debt," he finally said.

"You owe me no debt," I said. "I am glad I was awake. Good night, sir."

"What! You *will* go?"

"I am cold, sir."

"Cold, yes. Go then."

But he did not release my hand. I didn't know what to do until I finally thought to say, "I hear Mrs. Fairfax."

At that, he released me and I went back to my room, though I could not rest. I felt feverish and confused. I wondered what would happen in the morning.

Visitors at Thornfield

Morning came and I didn't see Mr. Rochester at all. Servants bustled about Mr. Rochester's room, righting the damage. They all believed he had fallen asleep with a candle.

I was stunned to see Grace Poole sitting among them, calmly sewing a new pair of bed curtains. I couldn't imagine why she was still employed. If she were young and beautiful, I might believe she was a particular favorite of Mr. Rochester, but she was older than the master. Her face was square and lined.

All day I expected Mr. Rochester to call us to take tea with him. Finally, I joined Mrs. Fairfax in her room. She seemed happy to see me as always.

"It's a lovely night," she said. "Mr. Rochester has good weather for traveling."

I was surprised to hear he had left. I learned Mr. Rochester was away to visit his fashionable friends. He was unlikely to return for many days.

"His friends came here once," Mrs. Fairfax said. "They are very fine." Mrs. Fairfax spoke at length about the beautiful Miss Blanche Ingram. Miss Ingram was also very accomplished. "She and Mr. Rochester sang a duet," Mrs. Fairfax said, smiling at the memory. "It was a treat to hear them."

I left the kind lady's company as soon after that as I could. I felt nearly sick with the realization that I had grown unduly fond of Mr. Rochester. I hated the idea of him spending his time with a lady who was all the things I was not. Miss Ingram was fine and beautiful. I looked at my own plain face in the mirror and said, "How could you imagine Mr. Rochester thinks well of you?"

Ten days passed with no sign of Mr. Rochester's return. "He often goes straight from Leas to London and then to the Continent," Mrs. Fairfax said. "We may not see him for a year to come."

Then a note arrived that threw the house into a storm of activity. The master was returning in three days' time and he was bringing friends! Adèle's lessons were canceled since every hand was needed to help with cleaning and cooking.

Whenever I had the chance, I paid close attention to Grace Poole. I still felt deep concern that she was allowed to stay at Thornfield after nearly killing the master. My confusion grew when I overheard Leah chatting with one of the village girls hired to help with the cleaning.

"Grace Poole must be paid well," the village girl said.

"I wish I had as good," Leah answered. "And no one could do her job better. I'd not like to fill her shoes, not for twice the money she gets."

Then the village girl seemed to notice me as I scrubbed at a window glass. Her voice dropped still lower but I could hear it plain enough. "Does she know?"

Leah shook her head, glancing nervously at me. This left me with much to wonder about.

Finally the day came for the guests to arrive. The staff crowded the windows to watch the carriages. Only two people came on horseback. I recognized Mr. Rochester at once with Pilot running along beside his horse. The other horse carried a lady who could only be Blanche Ingram. Her fine riding clothes almost swept the ground and her raven curls bounced as she rode.

I quickly gathered Adèle to a classroom to keep her out from underfoot. We were soon forgotten with the needs of the visitors. The next day, Mrs. Fairfax told me that Adèle and I would be expected in the drawing room after dinner.

"Why would Mr. Rochester want me to come?" I said in surprise.

"I do not know, but he was insistent. I suggested you would find it uncomfortable," she said gently. "But he said he would fetch you if you don't come."

Then Mrs. Fairfax recommended that I go down while the rest were at dinner so that Adèle and I might find a quiet spot out of the way. We did so. Though none of the fine guests showed the least interest in me, several were kind to Adèle. The child was clearly delighted by the attention.

In their fine clothes, the women reminded me of bright, plumy birds. I paid particular attention to Miss Ingram. She was the most beautiful of the group, but she seemed scornful of the others. She was clearly accomplished, but treated her skills like a competition at which she must constantly win.

When the gentlemen joined the ladies, it was clear that Miss Ingram's attention was fully

upon Mr. Rochester and his upon her. I watched them closely as the beautiful lady preened and flirted with him. Finally the master stepped away from her, but she followed.

"I thought you were not fond of children," she said with a cold smile.

"I am not."

"Then what caused you to take charge of such a doll as that?" she asked, pointing toward Adèle.

"She was left on my hands," he said.

"You should send her to school," Miss Ingram said. "You would find it far less expensive than keeping a tiresome child and a detestable governess." At this she talked awhile on how much she disliked governesses. When not all of the young women agreed with her, she quickly changed the subject. She demanded Mr. Rochester sing a duet with her.

I enjoyed his voice very much, but slipped away by a side door as soon as they were done.

As I hurried to reach the quiet of my rooms, I ran into Mr. Rochester.

"Why did you not come and speak to me downstairs?" he asked.

"I did not wish to disturb you with your guests," I said.

"You look pale," he said. "What is the matter?"

"Nothing, sir."

"Then return to the drawing room. I want you there."

"I am tired, sir."

"More than that, you are near tears," he said. "If I had more time and privacy, I would learn why. But now I must let you go. I expect you to appear in the drawing room every evening. It is my wish. Good night."

Fortunes Told

The days that followed continued to be busy for the household. Each evening I took my place as watcher over the play of the guests. Each evening I saw clearly that Miss Ingram preferred Mr. Rochester. And each evening I saw how little she deserved him.

I was certain he intended to marry her. It was clear she intended to marry him. I believe I could have accepted this if I truly believed she could make him happy. I did not believe she would. She was all show and cold heart. He deserved better.

Whenever Mr. Rochester entered the room, I saw an immediate change in the group. It was as if he were the spark of life that created the party. Never was this more deeply felt than one day when he was called away on business.

The group grew so dull that Adèle took to staring out the window, hoping for Mr. Rochester's return. Finally she cried out, "There he is!"

Miss Ingram darted forward and peered out the window. "Why is he in a coach when he left on a horse?"

The coach door opened and the man who stepped out was clearly not Mr. Rochester. "Oh, you tiresome monkey!" Miss Ingram snapped at Adèle. "Who perched you in the window to call out foolish things?" Then she glared at me.

Directly after this, a tall, fine-looking gentleman entered and introduced himself as Mr. Mason. Upon hearing that the master was away, he announced he would stay. The group seemed to enjoy Mr. Mason's company very much.

Shortly after this, a servant came in to say that a gypsy woman had arrived at the house and refused to leave until she was given the chance to tell the fortunes of the fine ladies. Miss Ingram seemed to like this idea especially. The gypsy was shown into a room where each of the unmarried women would join her to hear her fortune.

Naturally, Miss Ingram went first. She returned with her mood clearly dampened. She would answer no questions about what the gypsy had said.

"She plays at fortune-telling, but I am not so foolish as to believe in her," she said.

The other ladies took their turns with the gypsy and returned in far higher spirits.

"She told us such things," one of the ladies said breathlessly. "She knows all about us."

"She even knew who we liked most in the world," another said.

The gentlemen then laughed and teased the ladies to tell them. Much blushing and stammering followed that. I enjoyed watching this play out. Then the servant came to my side. He told me the gypsy woman insisted there was one more unmarried lady and she would speak to her before she left.

"I thought it must be you," he said. "There is no one else for it. Will you come?"

I went. The woman sat in the library, bundled up in a cloak and a broad-brimmed hat. I warmed my hands by the fire, determined not to be the first to speak.

"Do you want your fortune told?" the woman asked in a harsh voice.

"If you like," I said. "I have no faith in your trade."

"Why don't you tremble?" she asked.

"I am not cold."

"Why don't you turn pale?"

"I am not sick."

"Why don't you believe in my art?"

"I am not silly."

"You are cold and sick and silly," the gypsy insisted. "You are cold because you are alone in the world. You are sick because you want love but it is held from you. And you are silly because you could have the happiness you seek if you only reached out for it."

"I believe you could say those things about anyone who lives dependent as I do," I said quietly.

The gypsy snorted. "Do you have nothing you wish for your future? Do you have hope?"

"I hope to save enough money to set up a school some day," I said. "I would like to be independent."

"You do not wish to marry?" she asked.

"It seems unlikely," I said.

"There is a marriage to come to this house," the gypsy said. "Your master is in love, is he not? He will be married soon."

"I did not come here to hear Mr. Rochester's fortune," I said. "I thought you would tell my own."

"I cannot see it. I know what you could have, but not what you will have," she said.

Something in the tone of this drew my attention. I stepped closer to the gypsy woman and peered at her. I recognized the face hidden in the shadows of the hat. At that moment, the figure rose and tossed off the cape. It was Mr. Rochester.

"The play is played out," he said.

"What a strange thing to do," I said, frowning. Then I remembered that I had news for him. "We have a guest that has come to see you. It is a Mr. Mason from the West Indies."

Mr. Rochester shuddered and sank back into the chair. "My little friend," he whispered, "I wish I were on a quiet island with only you. I wish trouble and danger were far from us."

"Can I help you, sir?" I asked.

"Tell Mr. Mason I would speak with him here," he said. "Then go on to your room."

I did as he asked. As I slipped away, I heard Mr. Rochester greet Mr. Mason so warmly that I thought all must now be well. I hurried to bed and to sleep.

Called Away

I was well asleep when a cry awoke me in the middle of the night. I hurried out into the hall where guests rushed about in great confusion. Mr. Rochester calmed them with a promise to find out what caused the sound.

I slipped back into my room and dressed quickly. Something told me the master might need me again. I was correct, for soon a light tapping came to my door.

"Am I wanted?" I asked.

The master answered. "Come with me. Bring a sponge from your washbasin and your smelling salts."

I brought them and hurried after the master. When we approached a closed door on the third floor, Mr. Rochester turned to me. "You don't turn sick at the sight of blood?"

"I think I shall not. I have never been tried."

"Give me your hand then," he said. I did. "It is warm and steady."

He led me into a dim chamber, where a man slumped in a chair. I recognized him as Mr. Mason, though he seemed pale and lifeless now. Mr. Rochester used my smelling salts and Mason moaned.

"I must go and fetch the doctor," Mr. Rochester said. "Until then, I need you to stay with him and sponge the blood like this." He demonstrated the task. "And use the smelling salts if he faints. Do not talk with him."

Then he looked into Mr. Mason's face. "Do not talk to her if you value your life."

As I tended the wounded man in the dark room, I heard sounds coming from the beyond the door that connected this room to another. I heard growls and snarls like an animal. Then I heard a voice I recognized as Grace Poole.

Time stretched out before me, but I stayed to my task and did not speak.

Finally, Mr. Rochester returned with Dr. Carter. "Dress the wound," the master insisted. "He must leave with you in half an hour. He has lost some blood, but it is a minor wound."

The doctor focused on the wound. "I can handle this easily enough. How is this? This looks like teeth marks."

"She bit me and said she would drink my blood," Mason gasped. "She looked so quiet at first. I did not expect it."

"I warned you," Mr. Rochester said with a shudder. "You should have waited until tomorrow when I would have gone with you."

"I thought I might do some good," Mason moaned.

Mr. Rochester sent me to check if anyone stirred below. When I returned to say the house still slept, he and the doctor helped Mr. Mason down through the house and outside to the doctor's carriage.

"Take care of him," the master said. "Keep him at your house until he is quite well. I will come to see him in a few days."

"Treat her well," Mason gasped.

"I do my best and I have done it and will do it," Mr. Rochester said.

Then the carriage took the doctor and his patient away.

"Thank you, Jane," Mr. Rochester said. "You have done me another good turn."

"I like to serve you, sir," I said.

"I can see you do," he said as he led me to a bench to sit with him. "Do you think that a mistake once made must be paid for without ending? Do you think a man who has done his best can reach for happiness if he knows himself blameless? Must a man be bound by the views and thoughts of others?"

I looked at him, unsure how to answer such mysterious questions. His questions seemed important to him and I wanted to answer well.

"I think these are questions better asked of God than me," I said finally.

Mr. Rochester sighed and looked out across the land. "Little friend, do you think Miss Ingram would help me be a better man if I married her?"

He looked at me closely then. "You've gone quite pale. I should not keep you away from your rest. Hurry off." And so I went, though I found little rest.

What I soon found was a visitor waiting for me. It was Robert Leaven, the coachman who had married Bessie. He told me Bessie was well with a new baby, but that the rest of the news was bad.

"Mr. John died a week ago yesterday," he said. "He had ruined his health and spent much of his mother's money in gambling debts. Now they say he killed himself."

I was silent, not knowing what to say in response to this.

"Mrs. Reed has been unwell for some time," Robert continued. "When she heard of her son's death, she had a stroke. She is not expected to live. She calls for you. I do not know why. I would like to take you to her tomorrow, if you will come."

"I will come," I said. I hurried off quickly in search of Mr. Rochester to ask leave to go. He was with his guests, but I knew I could not wait. Miss Ingram glared at me when I interrupted to call Mr. Rochester away.

"I need a leave of absence for a week or two. I must visit the wife of my uncle. She is dying and she calls for me," I said.

"I thought you had no relatives," he said.

"None that would own me. Mrs. Reed cast me off because I was poor and plain and she disliked me."

"Then why go to her? She would probably be dead by the time you reached her. I don't like you to go." He looked at my face a moment and sighed. "If you must go, promise you will only stay a week."

"I cannot. I do not know how long I will be needed," I replied.

Mr. Rochester clearly did not like my leaving but he finally agreed. He tried to give me fifty pounds, but I refused. I would not accept more than he would owe me for two years' wages! Finally he settled for giving me ten.

"There is more business we should discuss," I said. "I will need a new position when you are married. Miss Ingram has been clear on that. I need to know when to advertise."

"Advertise?" he said in surprise. "You'll not advertise. I'll take care of it, Jane. Just trust me."

I agreed to that and we parted, though reluctantly.

CHAPTER
10
Going Home

I reached the lodge of my aunt's estate in the late afternoon. Bessie greeted me with warmth. She told me that Mrs. Reed had improved slightly and might linger for a week or two more. She also warned me that my cousins were not enthusiastic about my visit. This hardly seemed surprising.

When I went to the main house, I found Eliza coldly silent. Georgiana seemed eager to talk but clearly scornful of my lower position. I found I liked neither one any better than I had when we were children.

As soon as I could, I went up to visit with Mrs. Reed. If I had hoped for any show of remorse from Mrs. Reed, I was disappointed.

She lay in bed, looking pale, sick, and stern. Her voice was cold when she spoke.

"I wish you to stay until we can talk some things over," Mrs. Reed said. "But not tonight. I find I have trouble remembering." Then her mind seemed to wander and she began to talk about me instead of to me. The words she said were not kind. Then she drifted into fretting about her son's gambling debts.

Bessie suggested I let Mrs. Reed rest and I did. My days fell into a quiet pattern. My cousins grew used to having me around and Georgiana even asked me to walk with her. Her conversation focused always on herself and her interests, but I didn't really mind.

Eliza still spoke little. She followed a rigid schedule of activity each day and seemed content in that. Neither Georgiana nor her sister visited their mother often, and Mrs. Reed spent most of her time alone.

Finally I visited Mrs. Reed again. "I am very ill," she said. "I cannot move a limb. I must

ease my mind before I die. I have twice done you wrong. I broke the promise to my husband to bring you up as my own child." She paused and her mouth twisted in distaste.

"I must get this over with," she said finally. "Three years ago, I received a letter from your uncle John Eyre in Madeira. He wanted to know you and to make you his heir. I never told you. I disliked you too much to want to see you so blessed."

She seemed to choke on emotion and I hurried to get her a sip of water.

"Mrs. Reed," I said, "think no more of this. Let it all pass from your mind. I would have been glad to love you if you had let me. I am content to forgive you now."

After that, Mrs. Reed faded fast. She died at midnight. I stayed a few days more to help my cousins and then hurried back to Thornfield.

I felt as if I were going home. I knew Mrs. Fairfax and little Adèle would be glad to see me again. But most of my thoughts were of seeing the master, even though I knew he must soon be married and gone from my sight.

I was so eager to hurry my trip that I walked the miles to the house instead of waiting for a carriage. As I crossed the fields, I saw the master leaning on a tree. He saw me at the same moment.

"Hallo!" he cried. "There you are! You've been absent a whole month and forgotten us."

I felt warmed by his words and tone. "Thank you, Mr. Rochester," I said. "I am strangely glad to get back again to you. Wherever you are is my home."

I hurried to the house then and to the welcome that was as warm as I expected. I returned to my duties at once, but the gloom of knowing my time was short made me sad and tired.

I rested poorly and often walked alone in the evenings. On one such walk, I came upon the master again. He called to me before I could slip away.

"So lovely a night," he said. "It is a shame to sit in the house. Thornfield is a pleasant place in summer, is it not?"

"Yes, sir."

"It is sad you must move on. You told me you would need a new position and I have found one. Adèle will go to school. Miss Ingram has helped me to find a place for you with a family in Ireland. You will teach their five daughters. They are warmhearted people."

"It is a long way off, sir," I whispered.

"From what, Jane?"

My voice came in airless gasps. "From England and from Thornfield and from *you*, sir." Tears came then. I did not sob, but I could not stop the overflow of tears.

"It is. I shall never see you again, Jane. I never go to Ireland," Mr. Rochester said. "We have been good friends, Jane, haven't we?"

"Yes, sir."

"I have the oddest feeling, my little friend," he said. "I feel as if a string is knotted under my left rib and it stretches to your tiny frame. When you go so far, I am afraid that cord will be snapped and I will bleed inside." He smiled sadly and shook his head. "You will forget me soon, of course."

"I never should, sir." I began to sob. "I grieve to leave Thornfield. I love it here. I have not been trampled on. I have not been buried with inferior minds. I have talked face-to-face with you. And when I think of leaving you, it is like looking at death."

"Then stay."

"I cannot," I sobbed. "Your bride."

"I have no bride," he said.

"But you will."

"I will," he agreed. "But it will not be Miss Ingram. I have given no promise. And she does not want me. A gypsy told her I have no real fortune and she has no more interest in me. I will marry soon, but it will not be to her."

"Then I still must go. I cannot stay while you marry. Do you think because I am poor, obscure, plain, and little that I have no soul or heart? You are wrong. I have as much soul as you and as much heart. If God had given me beauty as well, I would make it hard for you to send me away. As hard as it is for me to leave."

"Then stay," he said and gathered me in his arms and kissed me.

I pushed against him. "You are to be a married man. Let me go!"

"Jane, be still," he said, still holding me fast. "You struggle like a little bird tearing its feathers in desperation."

"I am no bird," I said. "No net holds me. I am a free human. And I want to be let go." I struggled free then.

"Then in freedom, you decide," he said. "I offer you my heart, my hand, and a share of all my possessions. Pass through life at my side as my second self and best earthly companion. It is only you I intend to marry. It was only ever you."

I stared at him, shocked and unbelieving.

"You doubt me, Jane?"

"Entirely."

"I love you. Say you will marry me."

"Then, sir, I will marry you," I said.

He held me again and said, "God pardon me and man meddle not with me. I have her and will hold her."

"There is no one to meddle, sir. I have no family to interfere."

We walked to the house then and the rain began, soaking us by the time we reached the door. Mr. Rochester kissed me again, just as Mrs. Fairfax passed by. I did not like her to think poorly of me. Mr. Rochester said he would make the announcement in the morning, and I knew she would be happy for me then. I went up to my room happier than I had ever been.

CHAPTER 11
A Wedding

Mr. Rochester made the announcement just as he said and I wrote a letter to Bessie and to my uncle, wanting to share my good news. Mr. Rochester called me away from the classroom to tell me he had ordered the family jewels for me to wear. Then he said he would take me to be fitted for new clothes as well.

"Oh, do not insist on such things," I cried. "I will feel foolish. You loved plain Jane, do you not intend to marry her?"

"You are a beauty in my eyes," he said.

"But not beauty enough. Already you seek to change me," I said. "I will allow some new clothes but no jewels. And I will continue as Adèle's governess until the time comes for the wedding. We can talk each evening if you like, as we always have."

"Your request is granted for the time," he finally agreed.

"Now I have something to ask of you," I said. "Why did you pretend that you intended to marry Miss Ingram?"

"I knew you liked me," he said. "But I am older than you and not handsome. I thought perhaps if you were jealous, you would love me."

"That was a disgraceful way to behave," I scolded. I could tell it would not do to let Mr. Rochester rule over me. He would bully me and grow tired of meekness. So I spent the days until the wedding much as I always had. My chats with Mr. Rochester were often filled with small contests of will and wits. Still, it was a happy time.

I resisted the purchase of fancy clothes, though I did accept new dresses. They were plain but beautifully made. Soon all were packed away, for Mr. Rochester intended for us to take an extended trip after the wedding.

I looked at the trunk often, tracing the name "Mrs. Rochester." It seemed so strange. I would soon give away my name and everything I knew. I believed I would be happy, yet I felt unsettled.

Then close to the day of the wedding, Mr. Rochester went away to settle business matters. On his return, I met him in a great state of distress.

"What is it, Jane?" he asked.

"The veil came," I said. "The fancy one you meant to surprise me with. I had made a small square to pin to my hair, but I could see you had other plans."

"And the veil makes you look so sad?" he said.

I shook my head. "After I went to bed, the wind howled in such a mournful way that I felt quite alone. Finally, I fell asleep and had a horrible dream of Thornfield. It had fallen to ruin. I looked for you and I heard your horse, but I could not find you. I awoke trembling."

"Is that all?" he asked, smiling. "A bad dream?"

I shook my head again. "On waking, I saw a person going through my wardrobe. It was a strange, tall woman with thick dark hair. She took the beautiful veil and tore it to bits. Then she came to my bedside and looked close in my face. She was like an animal, growling. I fainted."

"But Jane," he said. "It must have been a dream."

"Then why," I whispered, "did I wake to find the veil in bits on the floor?"

Mr. Rochester shuddered and threw his arms around me. "Thank God you are all right," he whispered. "Jane, I think it must have been Grace Poole."

"It was not," I said.

"I believe what you saw mixed with the dream in your mind," he said. "It had to be

Grace Poole. There is no other answer for it. You must sleep with Adèle tonight. Tomorrow we will be married and away from here."

I did not know how I felt about that, but I obeyed him. Morning came as it does. The church lay so close, we walked together to it. Somehow the stone building looked stern. I shivered in the shadow of it.

We joined the pastor at the altar and he began the service. When he reached the point where always the pastor asks if any object to the marriage, he barely paused. Who speaks at such a time? The question is always asked, but never answered.

Except, this time.

"The marriage cannot go on," a voice called from behind us. "Mr. Rochester is already married."

A man came forward and announced himself as an attorney from London. He had been sent by his client, John Eyre of Madeira, who was too ill to come himself. The lawyer

said he had a witness who could confirm that Mr. Rochester was married.

Mr. Mason came forward nervously.

Mr. Rochester grew pale as milk as Mr. Mason said he had seen Mr. Rochester's wife three months before. She had attacked him. Mr. Mason said the woman was his sister.

Finally Mr. Rochester held up his hand. "Jane Eyre knew nothing of my wife. She is innocent in this."

Then he commanded us to come to the house and see this wife. We went. As I expected, we climbed to the third floor and entered the chambers of Grace Poole. She was there, cooking over the fire, and she was not alone.

"She sees you," Grace said. "Take care, sir."

Someone paced the far end of the room. She bent over so far, she nearly crawled on all fours. Black hair hung over her face and she cried and moaned. It was the creature I had seen in my room.

The mad woman rose up and rushed at Mr. Rochester. She clawed and bit, but he never hurt her. He pushed the woman into a chair and bound her with ropes. Finally he led us out of the room.

"That is my wife," Mr. Rochester said. "Can you blame me for seeking another?" Then he left us.

"Your uncle will be glad to hear you were spared," the attorney said. "He received your letter and knew of Mr. Rochester. He is too ill to respond himself and that is why he sent me. I am glad I was in time."

I do not know what I answered. I do not know if I answered. I walked to my room, collapsed on my bed, and cried until I could cry no more.

Escape

When I awoke, I discovered that Mr. Rochester had not given up the thought of being with me. He begged me to forgive him. This I did at once. He bent to kiss me and I turned away.

"You will not love me?" he said. "Because I have a wife already?"

"Yes."

"You intend to leave me?"

"I must. Adèle must have a new governess."

"Adèle will be sent to school," he said. "Then we can leave. You and I. I know you could not stay here with me. I would not ask that of you. We can go. I have a place we can go."

I shook my head.

"Jane you must see reason!" he cried. "We can be together somewhere far from here.

Pointing fingers and wagging tongues won't touch us. Stop shaking your head, don't you love me?"

"I do love you," I said. "Though this is the last time I will say it. I must leave."

"Because of a madwoman in my attic?" he demanded. "A woman who has never loved me. A woman who has never been a wife to me. My father and brother tricked me into the marriage for the sake of money. She was beautiful then and I was too young to know what a fool I was being. I barely spoke to her before the wedding and afterward, it was too late. I brought her here and hired Grace Poole to watch over her. She's clever and dangerous. But she is not a wife to me."

"But still your wife is living," I said calmly. "You must not think to take another."

"I did think it. I have thought of nothing else since that frosty winter afternoon when I saw a quiet little figure sitting by herself. It would not go away until I was helped. I knew then that I must get you to love me."

"And I do," I said.

"You see then? We must be together. It is right and good."

I felt sure that if I gave in he would grow tired of me. Something would break then. The end could not be right with such a beginning. So I begged to go and rest. He insisted we would talk more in the morning, but he let me go.

I rose early, before dawn. I gathered those few things I considered truly mine into a small parcel. I left all the presents he had bought me. Those were for his wife, and I could not be his wife.

I took a few small loaves of bread and a bottle of water from the kitchen. Then I slipped out the door and walked to Millcote as quickly as my legs could go. I gave a coachman what little money I had and he carried me two days down the road. I ate only what I had carried with me.

The coachman set me out in a place called

Whitcross. In my hurry to move on, I left my parcel in the carriage. I had no money and only the clothes I wore. I looked for work, but who would hire someone that no one knew? I could give no references. I had no friends.

I slept outside and for food, I had only what kind folks would give me. I had become a beggar and it was not enough. I could feel my strength slipping away each day. I walked and walked.

Finally, one evening I came to a tiny cottage where I could see three figures through a window. Two young women sat in low rocking chairs. A large old dog lay at their feet. An old woman sat at the hearth, knitting a stocking. The scene was so warm and snug, I longed to be part of it.

I went to the door and knocked. The old woman answered but when I begged to come in, she sent me away. She thought I was a beggar or a thief. I collapsed near the door, the last of my strength gone.

"I will die," I said. "I believe in God. I will wait for His will."

"All men must die," a voice said. "But you will not perish of want this day."

"Who speaks?" I cried, for I could not see in the murky darkness. Instead of answering, a dark figure swept by me and knocked at the door.

"Is that you, Mr. St. John?" the old woman said from the other side of the door.

"Yes, yes, open quickly," he called.

The door swung open and the old woman said, "'Tis a wild night and bad folks are around. A beggar woman was here. Oh, she lies here still. Off with you!"

"Hush, Hannah!" the man cried. "I will talk with this young woman." He called me to come with him and I obeyed with difficulty. My head swam and I dropped into the first chair I came upon. The two young ladies fussed over me kindly and fed me bread dipped in milk.

St. John asked me where I came from and who they might call to help me. I told them

I had no one. I told them my name was Jane Elliot, as I dared not give my real name and make a trail for Mr. Rochester to follow. They soon saw I was too tired for questions and sent me off to a warm bed, where I slept in grateful joy.

When I awoke, I started a new part of my life. None of the kind family who had taken me in normally lived in the house. St. John was a village parson and Hannah worked for him. His sisters Diana and Mary both worked as governesses in London. They were gathered because of the recent death of their father, John Rivers.

The Rivers family was not rich, but they cared for me kindly and shared what they had without restraint. They accepted that I had secrets I must not share, though St. John might have pressed me if not for the scolding of his sisters. Even Hannah grew kinder to me.

Though I told them no names, I did relate that I was an orphan and had been trained as a

teacher by the Lowood Orphan Asylum. I said I had become a governess but had to flee my position because of a great calamity.

"I want to work," I said. "I will shun no honest work as soon as I am well enough to set my hand to it."

"If such is your spirit," St. John said, "I promise to help you in my own time and way."

And so I rested and grew strong. Shortly before the time when the Rivers family must scatter again to their jobs, they received a letter. A distant uncle had died, their last living relative. He was a wealthy man, but had left them nothing.

"Ah well," Mary said. "It makes us no worse off than we were before."

I came to love Diana and Mary like sisters, and we were all sad when the time came for them to return to London and their work. St. John would be returning to his work as well. I asked him if he had heard of any work I might undertake, since it was clear I needed a position now.

"In Morton, I have opened a village school for boys," he said. "I would like to open a second for girls. I need a teacher. The pay will be poor, but it comes with a small cottage that will be yours."

I accepted the offer promptly.

"Be sure you understand," he said. "These will be poor girls. They need only simple skills."

Again I agreed. And so it was settled.

CHAPTER 13
A New Family

I began my new life in the tiny cottage and taught the village girls. I was pleased to see the girls had a strong desire to learn, though their manners were rough. As my students grew in skills, I grew in familiarity with the village. I was touched by the generosity and good hearts of the farmers.

I devoted myself to the job, but still I was not happy. I felt restless, but I tamed my nature.

I learned that the village schools were partly funded by the richest man in the area. His daughter visited often and even taught a little class for the girls.

St. John came often to check on me. I quickly saw that the beautiful young woman was fond of St. John and he was desperately in love with her.

She was kind and we quickly became friends. I decided to sketch a portrait of her as a gift.

St. John came to see me while I was working on the portrait. He stared at it as if bewitched. I decided to talk with him about his love for the girl. Why did he not marry her? Clearly her father would approve and she was agreeable.

"I have a calling to the mission field," he said. "I have long postponed it, but I will go. And when I go, I must have a wife who can withstand the challenge or no wife at all. Can you picture Miss Rosamond as a missionary's wife?"

I had to admit I could not. "But you love her. Do you not do God's work here and now?"

"To be a missionary is dearer to me than the blood in my veins. It is what I live for," he said.

St. John drew a sheet of paper to cover the portrait. It was the sheet I tested my pens on. St. John suddenly started and bent to stare at the paper. I could not imagine what had caught his interest. He tore the corner from the sheet, slipped it into his pocket, and left.

He returned to visit again a few days later. "I have a story to tell you," he said. He began his tale and I felt fear clutch at my heart. It was my story. He told me of an orphan sent to live with the Reed family, of her time at the school, and of her work at Thornfield. He finished with the sad events of Mr. Rochester's mad wife and the near wedding.

"Mr. Rochester must have been a bad man," he said.

"You don't know him," I said. "So don't pronounce an opinion on him."

"Very well," he said. Then he pulled a slip of paper out of his pocket. It was the torn corner and I saw I had written my name—my true name.

"I know something else of you, Jane Eyre," he said. "Your uncle in Madeira has died and left you all his property. You are rich." Then he smiled. "You actually heard of this man's death once before. He was also our uncle. Your father was my mother's brother."

Tears gathered in my eyes. "We are cousins?"

"We are cousins, yes," St. John replied.

I could hardly contain my joy. I had been an orphan and now I had a family. I made a decision at once. I would divide the inheritance four ways. We would all benefit! Mary and Diana need not be governesses. And St. John could begin as a missionary whenever he liked.

St. John resisted the idea of dividing my inheritance at first, but I stayed firm. Diana and Mary were called from London. I gave up my place as village teacher and another was found. Diana, Mary, and I moved into John Rivers's old house and we lived with great pleasure.

St. John threw himself into his studies in preparation for leaving to the mission field. He asked me to learn Hindustani with him so that he might have someone to help him strengthen his understanding. I agreed.

I soon found him a rigid taskmaster. He was never cruel, but his praise was rare and his disapproval cold. I found more and more of my effort was directed toward pleasing him. That part of me that was strong and defiant seemed to shrink smaller and smaller. I felt as if I were losing myself in his unbending personality.

His sisters scolded him for pushing me so hard, but he only said, "Jane is not such a weakling as you would make her. She could bear whatever came her way."

During this time, I wrote several letters to Mrs. Fairfax. I had to know if Mr. Rochester was well. I received no response. This worried me, but I had little time for my own thoughts as St. John pushed me to help him with his work.

Finally, he asked me to walk with him one day. "Jane, I leave in six weeks. Come with me to India as my wife and fellow laborer."

I was stunned. "I have no vocation, no call to such a task."

"All have the call," he said firmly. "You are designed to be a missionary's wife. I have observed you. You are the right choice."

"I would go with you," I said. "I would put my hand to the task, but I will not be your wife. Let me go as your sister, but not your wife."

He was resolute. I would be his wife. I knew this was something I could not do. To be married to St. John would kill me.

Still, he pressed and his disapproval was a cold thing. I could feel myself weakening, even as I knew it would mean my death. It grew harder and harder to say no.

One day as St. John listed again the reasons why God demanded I do as he said, I was startled by another voice calling me from outside.

"Jane! Jane! Jane!" The voice was filled with pain and longing. It was a voice I knew, for it could only be Mr. Rochester.

"I am coming!" I cried. I ran outside and searched, but no one was there. I knew I must return to Thornfield. My master needed me and no one would stand in my way.

CHAPTER
14
A Dream

I arose at dawn to begin my trip. I found a note under my door from St. John. He remarked on my odd behavior the day before and reminded me again that he hoped I would change my mind and answer God's call to marry him. I set the note aside without a thought.

At breakfast, I told Diana and Mary that I was going on a journey that would last some days. They fretted over my traveling alone but did nothing to delay me. I left that afternoon.

After two days on the coach, the landscape began to look familiar. We stopped to water the horses at an inn and I asked, "How far is Thornfield Hall from here?"

"Two miles across the fields."

I struck out across the fields, hungry to see Thornfield again. In my mind, I could picture its bold, simple lines. I imagined looking up at the master's window and seeing him standing there.

I reached the wall by the orchard and crept up to the gate. I peeked around the tall stone pillar and what I saw took my breath away. I now knew why no one answered letters to Thornfield. The stately house was the burned ruin from my dream.

I ran across the lawn and crept along the fire-blackened stones. Then I hurried back to the inn. I had to learn what had happened.

The innkeeper knew Thornfield well. "I was the late Mr. Rochester's butler," he said.

My heart nearly stopped. Was Mr. Rochester dead? But then the innkeeper went on, and I realized he had been the butler for my master's father. He told me the fire had been set by the mad Mrs. Rochester in the middle of the night.

"She set it in the room the governess had stayed in," he said. "She was mad, but perhaps she knew that the master had loved that girl. She was a little thing and plain, so I hear. The master turned quite the hermit when she ran off."

I nodded and the man went on. Mr. Rochester had wakened from the smoke. He'd insisted that everyone get out of the house, but Mrs. Rochester had fled to the roof.

"She stood, waving her arms and shouting," the innkeeper said. "I saw her myself."

He told me that the master would not leave her. But before he could reach her, she threw herself off the roof and died. Then when the master tried to escape the house, he was trapped in falling wreckage.

"But he is alive?" I whispered.

"Yes, though it might have been better if he had not lived," the man said. "He is blind and he lost a hand in the fire."

"Is he in England?" I asked.

The man nodded. "At the manor house in Ferndean," he said. "It's a desolate spot. Two servants from Thornfield live with him, John and Mary."

I then offered the man twice his usual hire if he would drive me to Ferndean. He did, dropping me about a mile from the house.

Night was falling by the time I reached the house. I saw a man standing just outside the door and recognized Mr. Rochester at once. I stopped, and watched him silently.

My master looked so sad and lost. Finally John came out and called him in. Mr. Rochester refused the servant's arm but groped his way back to the house. I waited a bit before following.

John and Mary recognized me at once. They listened to my story of all that had passed since I fled Thornfield. I told them I would stay there. Then when the master rang, Mary told me he always called for candles in the evening along with a glass of water.

"Give the tray to me," I said. "I will carry it."

The parlor looked gloomy with only the light from the fire. Pilot spotted me and bounded forward, almost knocking the tray from my hands. I patted him and told him softly to lie down.

"Give me the water, Mary," Mr. Rochester called. I brought him the glass, with Pilot still dancing around me.

"Down, Pilot!" I said as I handed the glass to Mr. Rochester.

He froze. "Is that you, Mary?"

"Mary is in the kitchen," I answered.

He put out his hand and caught mine. "I know this voice and these small fingers. Is it Jane? Am I dreaming again? I dream of Jane often."

"I am Jane Eyre," I said. "I have found you and come back to you."

"But you may be a dream," he said.

I kissed his sightless eyes. I swept the shaggy hair from his forehead and kissed that, too.

"I thought you dead," he said.

"No, sir," I said. "I am an independent woman now. My uncle in Madeira is dead and left me his fortune. And I have cousins! I may come and go as I please."

"And you will stay with me?"

"Certainly. I will be your nurse, your housekeeper. I will read to you and walk with you. You will not be alone as long as I live."

He took so long to answer that I suddenly feared I had killed his feelings for me by being gone so long. Would he still want me for a wife?

"But you must marry someday," he said. "You are young and now wealthy. Why would you stay with a sightless block like me?"

"I am only in danger of loving you too much," I said.

I called then for supper and he asked me many questions about the time we had been apart. I answered each honestly until I was too weary to speak. Then I promised to tell more in the morning.

The next day, I took Mr. Rochester out for a walk. His questions for the day centered on St. John.

"This cousin of yours," he said, "do you like him?"

"He is a good man, sir," I said. "I could not help liking him."

"A good older man?"

"He is about twenty-nine, sir."

"But he is a man of little depth of wit?"

"No, sir, his brain is first-rate," I said. "He is polished and well-educated."

"But plain and bony?" Mr. Rochester asked.

"He is a handsome man," I said. "He is tall with blue eyes."

"And you would rather be with him?" Mr. Rochester asked, his voice angry. "Perhaps he will choose you for his wife."

"He already has, sir," I said. "He asked me to marry him several times."

"Then you must leave me," he said. "He will be a better husband than I."

"No," I said. "I will never leave you. St. John does not love me. He loves only the mission field. He asked me to be his wife because he thought I would be a good missionary. There is no love there. Would I ever marry for less than love?"

"You do not love him?"

"Only as family," I said.

"Jane, will you marry me?" Mr. Rochester asked.

"Yes, sir. I love you even more now than ever before," I replied.

And so, Reader, I married him. We had a quiet wedding. I wrote to my family immediately. Diana and Mary were delighted.

St. John was not. But he left for the mission field and worked the rest of his life at the task he loved most in the world.

I moved Adèle to a school close by so she could come home often and be with us. She grew up to be a fine lady.

Mr. Rochester began to recover much of his sight. He could never see to read, but he could see our son when he was born.

My Edward and I, then, are happy. And the more so, because those we most love are happy likewise. Diana and Mary Rivers are both married. Once every year, they come to see us or we go to see them. Diana's husband is a captain in the navy, a gallant officer and a good man. Mary's is a clergyman, a college friend of her brother's, and worthy of the connection. Both Captain Fitzjames and Mr. Wharton love their wives, and are loved by them.